ISBN 0 85079 110 3

RUPERT

A DAILY EXPRESS PUBLICATION

© EXPRESS NEWSPAPERS LTD. 1981
Printed in Great Britain

£1.80

"Your trowel is nowhere to be found,"
Frowns Rupert, searching all around

"Hi!" Bingo, Rupert's brainy chum,
To show his new machine has come.

"What can Daddy be up to?" wonders Rupert one bright summer day. In the garden Mr. Bear is busy lifting flower-pots and seed-boxes, peering under them and shaking his head. Rupert goes out to see if he can help. "What are you looking for?" he asks. "My trowel, my good garden trowel," Mr. Bear says. "It must be somewhere in the garden but I can't find it." So Rupert joins in the hunt for the missing trowel. But though he spends a long time looking under bushes and flowers, the trowel is nowhere to be found. "Don't worry," Rupert tells his Daddy, "It's bound to turn up." "I hope so," sighs Mr. Bear. "It's my favourite and I do so need it." Just then someone opens the garden gate and peeps round it. "Why, it's Bingo!" cries Rupert as he spies his chum, the brainy pup. Bingo is carrying something. "I've got my new invention here," he calls.

the CASTLE TRAP

The Squire is trapped by crooks. But Rupert, Bingo and Rollo save him with the help of Bingo's new treasure-tracer machine.

Says Mr. Bear, "What is it for?
Some novel way to sweep the floor?"

"The bulb lights up if metal's there.
We'll find your trowel around somewhere."

"A new invention!" exclaims Rupert. "Oh, come on in and let's have a look." Bingo who is very proud of his inventions is only too pleased to show this one off. It is round and flat with a light bulb and wires on top. It has a place where a long handle can be fitted. Rupert and his Daddy study it?" "What is it?" asks Mr. Bear. "A carpet-sweeper?" Bingo laughs. "Goodness, no. It's for finding hidden treasure," he says.

"Buried treasure!" gasps Rupert. "But how on earth does it work?" "It's really quite simple," says Bingo. "Let me show you." He fixes the handle to the machine and presses a switch. At once it begins to hum. He passes it backward and forward over the grass. "If there's anything made of metal under the ground the bulb will light up," he says. "Will it find Daddy's lost trowel?" asks Rupert. "Of course it will," chuckles Bingo.

RUPERT FINDS THE TROWEL

The bulb begins to glow. "You're right!
It's here!" calls Rupert with delight.

Smiles Mr. Bear, "Yes, you may go
To trace some treasure with that glow."

The chums leave Rupert's Dad behind,
Telling of Bingo's clever find.

"There's Rollo! I know what we'll do!
We'll show him your invention, too!"

Suddenly the bulb on the machine glows as it passes near a flower bed. "Try here," says Bingo. Rupert stoops, parts the leafy plants—and there is Mr. Bear's trowel! "Bingo's found it, Daddy!" shouts Rupert. Mr. Bear is delighted to have his favourite trowel again and can't thank the brainy pup enough. "Well," Bingo says. "I'm off now to see if I can trace some real treasure." "Oh, may I go too?" begs Rupert. Mr. Bear smiles, "Yes," he says. "But do be careful, both of you."

So the chums set off on their treasure hunt, leaving Mr. Bear to tell Constable Growler how his trowel was found by Bingo's invention. "Where do you think we should begin?" Rupert asks. "It'll have to be outside the village," Bingo says. "We can't go digging up people's gardens." So they make for the open country beyond Nutwood. Then suddenly Rupert points ahead. "Look, Rollo the gipsy boy and his caravan. Let's tell him about our treasure hunting idea, shall we?"

RUPERT MEET HIS GIPSY CHUM

Rollo and Granny turn to gaze.
"It's Rupert and Bingo," Rollo says.

Now Rollo's full of interest.
He cries, "Let's put it to the test!"

Bingo walks slowly up and down.
"Nothing so far." He gives a frown

Beneath the caravan they duck.
"The light's come on! I say, what luck!"

Rollo and his old Granny have just chosen their camping ground for the summer. The boy hears the chums' voices and looks up. "Why, it's Rupert!" he cries. "And Bingo, too." Soon the pup is busy showing the gipsy folk his invention. "It works," says Rupert and goes on to tell how it found his Daddy's trowel. "Now," he adds, "we're going to search for hidden treasure." But Granny is very suspicious of the box. "Don't trust things that I can't rightly understand," she mutters.

Unlike his Granny Rollo is keen to see how the invention works. So once more Bingo prepares his machine and Rupert and Rollo look on excitedly as he passes it slowly over the ground. But nothing happens and Bingo is just about to give up when he remembers he hasn't tried under the caravan. The moment he pokes his machine between the wheels the bulb lights up. "Oh, look!" exclaims Rupert. "That means that there must be something made of metal in the ground!"

RUPERT IS DISAPPOINTED

"Here's Daisy," Rollo says with pride.
"She'll pull the caravan aside."

The great horse moves the caravan.
"Let's dig as quickly as we can!"

They use two spades and dig until
A chinking sound gives them a thrill.

"A rusty can, not fit to keep!
A kettle! It's a rubbish heap!"

What can it be that Bingo's machine has found under Rollo's caravan? The chums can hardly wait to find out. "Maybe it's a hoard of gold," says Rollo excitedly. "Come on, we'll move the caravan and start digging." So they hurry to Daisy the horse tethered nearby and start harnessing her to the caravan. Within a few minutes Rollo shouts, "Gee up!" and Daisy pulls the caravan away from the spot. "Tcha!" mutters Granny. "You'll have no luck with that machine thing, I tell you."

But Rollo is not to be put off by his Granny's words. He fetches two spades and he and Rupert start digging up the ground where the caravan has been standing. Granny gives a mocking laugh and says. "You'll find nothing there." But presently they hear a chink as their spades hit something hard. They dig faster. But in the end all their treasure turns out to be is an old kettle and a rusty can. It's just an old rubbish heap. "Ha! Told you that thing's no good!" jeers Granny.

RUPERT GOES TO THE CASTLE

"A castle is the place to find
The treasure that you have in mind."

"That ruin is the one to try.
I'll join you later. Now, goodbye!"

Beside the moat the brainy pup
Begins, but that bulb won't light up.

Upon the drawbridge Bingo tries.
"Oo, look! It's glowing!" Rupert cries.

Rupert and Bingo are so disappointed that they are ready to give up. But Rollo won't hear of it. "No, you must try somewhere else," he says. "I know just the place." And he leads the pals to a high slope from which they can see the ruins of a castle. "You'd be likely to find relics there," says Rollo. The pals cheer up. "That sounds a good plan," they agree. "Let's all go and try." But Rollo has to finish putting the caravan in order. "I'll join you later," he promises.

So Rupert and Bingo go on alone to the ruined castle. "I'm glad Rollo thought of this," Bingo says as they pause beside the moat to make ready for the search. "We might find old armour or even swords." He switches on his machine and the two chums start into the castle. But they are still on the drawbridge when the bulb lights up, "I say, there must be some metal object in the water under the bridge," whispers Rupert. "Yes, but we can't go diving for it," chuckles Bingo.

9

RUPERT AND BINGO GET A SHOCK

They cross the drawbridge and begin
To search the courtyard, just within.

They stop beside an opening, for
The light's begun to glow once more.

A motorcycle is the cause.
'Who left it here?" The two chums pause.

The pals are startled by a shout.
Two strange men yell, "Be off! Get out!"

As soon as the pals cross the drawbridge into the ruined castle the light on Bingo's invention goes out. They find themselves in a courtyard. "We'll start here," Bingo says, starting to move his machine from side to side. "Then we can try some of the rooms —Hey, what's this?" At that moment the pals are passing a small opening in the stonework. The bulb is glowing again. "It looks like a sort of passage," says Rupert, peering into the dim opening. "Let's go in and see."

Behind the glowing bulb, the pals venture into the passage. But after a short way it ends in a blank wall. Then in one corner they spy a motorcycle. "Ah, so that's what made the light go on," Rupert whispers. "But whose is it?" The mystery of the motorcycle and the darkness make the pals feel suddenly nervous. They make their way back to the courtyard. Then—"Clear off! Get out!" An angry shout rings out. The chums wheel round to see two strangers glaring from the tower.

RUPERT'S GIPSY CHUM TURNS UP

The chums, forgetting to retrieve
Their treasure-tracer, quickly leave.

"Who could they be, those horrid men?"
Asks Bingo when they're safe again.

"Behind those bushes we can hide.
Then when they've gone we'll slip inside."

"Hello, you two! What's going on?
And where's your treasure-tracer gone?"

For a moment the pals are too startled to do anything. Then as the strangers brandish their fists, they take to their heels and make a dash for the drawbridge, leaving Bingo's invention in the courtyard. They stop only when they are once more clear of the castle. "Whew! At least they aren't chasing us!" pants Bingo. "What was that all about?" Rupert gasps. "We weren't doing any harm to them or anything else." "Well, whoever they are, I don't fancy going in there again," says Bingo. Then he gives a gasp of dismay as he realises that he has left his invention behind in the courtyard. "I daren't go back," he moans. "I know," says Rupert, "we'll hide in the bushes for a while. Maybe those men will go soon and we can go back for your treasure-tracer." So the chums keep watch from behind the bushes. But there is no sign of the men and they are about to give up when a voice makes them jump. "I thought you'd be at the castle!" It's Rollo.

RUPERT HEARS ABOUT THIEVES

"There've been some robberies round here.
Those men could be the thieves, I fear."

"The Squire! D'you think he knows that pair
Are lurking in the castle there?"

Says Rollo, "They may be his friends.
Let's wait and see how this thing ends."

"Let's move in closer silently
And hide where we can better see,"

"Ssh!" hisses Rupert. "Keep your voice down!" The gipsy boy looks in astonishment at the pals. "What's wrong?" he whispers, and Rupert tells him everything that has happened. "Strangers?" Rollo says with a soft whistle. "There have been one or two robberies in the village recently . . . I wonder if these two . . . perhaps this is where they bring their loot." The chums' eyes pop. But before they can say anything, Rollo points at the tall figure of a man approaching the castle. "It's the Squire!" he gasps. "What's he doing here?" The chums watch the old gentleman pause at the draw-bridge then stride into the castle. "I say, shouldn't we warn him about those men?" Rupert whispers. But Rollo says, "We can't be sure they are robbers. They could be friends the Squire has arranged to meet here. We don't want to look silly." Rupert and Bingo are still anxious so Rollo says, "All right, we'll keep watch from the bushes near the moat. Come on. Follow me!"

RUPERT SEES THE MEN LEAVE

They watch the gate from where they hide,
But nothing seems to stir inside.

An engine roars, the men appear.
They're leaving on their own, it's clear.

The pals dash through the castle hall.
"Oh, Squire are you all right?" they call.

Bingo's invention's where it stood.
"Is it damaged? No! That's good!"

Led by Rollo the chums wriggle through the thick undergrowth and soon they are in a new hiding place close to the moat. They watch in silence for a long time but still nothing happens. "The Squire and those men are still in there," Rupert whispers. "What can be happening?" Then all at once the silence is shattered by the roar of an engine and the motorcycle with the two strangers on it, dashes across the drawbridge and off down the track. "Where are they off to?" demands the gipsy boy.

"And where's the Squire?" asks Bingo. The moment the men are out of sight the pals dash into the castle. "Hello, Squire! Are you there? Can you hear us?" they call from the courtyard. But there is no answer. "I don't like this one bit," Bingo says as they venture further into the ruins. He spots his invention just where he left it. He tries it. "Good," he murmurs. "At least it's not damaged." Rupert frowns and says, "Why did those men dash off, and where's the Squire?"

RUPERT FETCHES THE TRACER

"The Squire has vanished. This is grim.
It's up to us to look for him."

Then down some stone steps Rupert's led.
"You stay just here. I'll go ahead."

"The Squire is here, shut in! Do bring
Bingo's invention, that's the thing!"

So Rupert dashes off at speed
To fetch the tracer that they need.

"Well, we know that Squire hasn't left the castle, so he must be somewhere in here," Rollo says. "I think it's up to us to find him." "Yes, but what if the two men come back," wonders Rupert. Bingo has the answer: "I'll keep watch while you two search." So while Bingo mounts guard, Rupert and Rollo head for the underground parts of the old castle. Half way down some stairs Rollo pauses and says, "I'm sure this leads to the vaults. You stay here, Rupert, and I'll go ahead."

Rollo vanishes into deep shadow leaving the little bear on the stairs. But he is soon back and waving excitedly. "I've found the Squire!" he calls. "He's locked up. Hurry back and fetch Bingo's machine." Without waiting to ask what the machine is wanted for, Rupert dashes back to the courtyard. Bingo has gone up to the battlements to watch for the men, but his invention is still where he left it. "I won't bother, Bingo," Rupert thinks. "I'm sure I can work this myself."

RUPERT FINDS THE KEY

*"Concealed beneath a stone or rock,
We'll find the key to fit that lock."*

*"I overheard those men tell where
The key is hidden, little bear."*

*Sweeping the tracer to and fro,
Rupert waits for the bulb to glow.*

*Beneath a stone he finds the key.
"Now we can set the Squire free!"*

Rupert picks up Bingo's treasure tracer and off he dashes downstairs. Rollo is waiting for him at the corner of a passage. "Good! Bring it here," he calls. He leads Rupert to a stout door. There is a barred window in it and peering through it is the Squire himself. "Ah, Rupert," he says. 'I have just been telling Rollo how those men trapped me. The door's locked but I overheard one of the men tell the other to hide the key under a stone." "We'll soon find it with Bingo's gadget," Rollo tells the old gentleman. Remembering how Bingo did it, Rupert switches on the machine and begins passing it over the passage floor, pausing beside every likely stone. All the while he watches the bulb. Suddenly it bursts into light. "I think. . ." begins Rupert. "Yes," he cries as he turns over a piece of fallen masonry. "Here it is!" And he holds up an old iron key. "We've found the key!" Rollo calls to the Squire. "We'll have you free in a moment—thanks to Bingo's gadget!"

RUPERT HEARS ABOUT A PLOT

The door swings open with a click.
"Bravo!" the Squire cries. "That was quick!"

"In answer to this note you came?
Then you were pounced on? What a shame!"

"The men are coming into sight!"
Calls Bingo, watching from a height.

"We'll deal with them!" exclaims the Squire.
"This gadget is what we require."

Eagerly Rollo tries the key, and although the lock is stiff he manages to turn it. There is a click and the heavy door creaks open. "Bravo!" cries the Squire. "I really am thankful to be out of that dreadful room." When they are back in the courtyard again the Squire shows the chums a note. "This was the note I received," he says. "It is unsigned and simply asks me to come at once to the castle. When I arrived those two men pounced on me and locked me in that cell." "But why would they want to do that?" asks Rupert. "To get me away from my house, I'm certain," the Squire says grimly. "They're probably robbing it at this very minute." Before he can go on there is a cry from Bingo: "They're coming! I can see their motorbike in the distance!" "Oo, we can still escape if we hurry," gasps Rupert. But the Squire smiles and shakes his head. "No, we'll prove a match for the two of 'em." He takes Bingo's machine and adds: "They'll have a taste of their own medicine!"

RUPERT FINDS WHAT'S NEEDED

"A bit of metal left below
Will make the gadget's light-bulb glow."

"The light will stay on in the gloom,
And lure the men into this room."

They hear the motorcycle's roar
And quickly hide themselves once more.

The engine stops then Rollo comes;
The Squire and Rupert join the chums.

Followed by the wondering chums, the Squire carries Bingo's treasure-tracer to a small room off the courtyard. "We'll lay the trap here," he says. "Now, I want you to look around for a piece of metal—something small." Almost at once Rupert finds a rusty bolt. "Will this do?" he asks. "It is just what we need," cries the Squire. At that moment Bingo returns in time to hear the Squire explain: "We'll leave the bolt under the machine so that the light stays on. Those rogues will be sure to wonder what is causing the glow and that will lure them into this room." The sound of the motorcycle gets louder. "The men must not see us," says the Squire. He asks Rupert to stay with him and sends Rollo and Bingo to hide by the gate and keep watch. Anxiously, the four friends wait for the men to ride into the courtyard. But suddenly the noise of the motorcycle stops. Then Rupert whispers, "Look, Rollo's waving to us. I wonder what can have happened."

RUPERT AND THE SQUIRE WATCH

One man is carrying a sack.
He says, "We'll sort this and go back."

The men stride past the hidden group
And on across the yard they troop.

"That's good!" The Squire then whispers low.
"They've noticed the invention's glow."

Then edging forward, he prepares
To trap the two men unawares.

Rupert and the Squire leave their hiding place and steal across the courtyard to where Bingo and Rollo are waiting. The two men have stopped their motorcycle on the other side of the drawbridge. One of them swings a heavy sack over his shoulder and they start towards the castle. "That was an easy haul, Jeff," laughs one as they reach the drawbridge. "We'll go back for some more as soon as we've sorted this lot." Silently the Squire and the chums slip into the shadows as the men enter the courtyard. Now, will they notice that light? The Squire steals carefully after them and Rupert follows. Suddenly the men stop. "Hey," growls one of them. "What's going on?" They have seen the glow from Bingo's machine. As they dump the sack and creep into the room where the light is, the Squire starts to edge along towards the doorway. Rupert is trembling with excitement as he looks on. "What is the Squire going to do?" he wonders. "Ah, I think I see . . ."

RUPERT HELPS THE SQUIRE

The Squire slams the door closed but
He needs a bar to keep it shut.

He thrusts the bar from wall to wall.
"Now we must fetch help first of all."

"I must have proof. I thought as much!
My silver trinklets, gold and such."

"I'll fetch our P.C. Growler, Quick,
That motorbike should do the trick!"

At that very moment the Squire leaps forward and slams shut the door of the room. "Quick!" he shouts. "Rupert! Rollo! Fetch a bar of wood!" The chums snatch up the biggest piece of timber they can find and rush it to the Squire who is grimly holding the door shut. Inside the room the two men are tugging at the door and shouting at the top of their voices. The Squire thrusts the stout wooden bar through the staple of the door and across from wall to wall. "That should keep them in until we get help," he pants. "Now off you go," he tells the three pals. "You will be safer out of the castle while I go for Constable Growler." But before they leave, the Squire takes a look inside the robber's sack. One glance is enough. "These are my valuables!" he exclaims. "I am going to fetch Constable Growler. I want you three to take the sack and hide in the bushes." And with that he starts across the drawbridge at a great pace. "Shan't be long!" he calls.

RUPERT HAS DOUBTS

*"That bar was old and none too strong.
It may not keep them in for long."*

*The Squire roars off, away he speeds.
The motorbike's just what he needs.*

*"To hold those men I'll try to raise
This ancient drawbridge," Rollo says.*

*Across the bridge the chums drag back
The stolen treasure in its sack.*

Rollo and Bingo start at once to drag the sack of valuables across the drawbridge. But Rupert hangs back. He is listening to the noise of the efforts being made by the two robbers to break out of the room. "Oh dear," he murmurs. "That piece of wood was awfully old. I really don't think it will keep them in for long." "I say, do come on, Rupert!" Rollo calls. "What's the matter?" As Rupert tells the others of his fears they hear the motorcycle start up. "It's the Squire!" exclaims Bingo. "No wonder he said he wouldn't be long!" As the Squire roars away Rollo says, "Rupert is right. That bar may not hold until the Squire is back with help." He thinks for a moment then he cries, "Got it! I'll stay in the castle and try to get the drawbridge up. That will keep those men in." "But, Rollo, you'll be trapped, too!" gasps Rupert. "I can look after myself," Rollo grins. But the other two are worried as he turns back and they drag the sack to safety.

RUPERT'S CHUM HAS TO SWIM

"If those men get out . . ." Rupert cries,
But now the drawbridge starts to rise.

Then Rollo gives a sudden shout:
"I'll have to jump! The men are out!"

Poised on the ledge he cries, "Here goes!"
The moat is deep enough, he knows.

"The men are trapped and at a loss.
I jammed the bridge so they can't cross."

Rupert and Bingo wait anxiously beside the moat after Rollo has disappeared back into the castle. "I do wish he hadn't stayed behind," Rupert says. "If those men escape and capture him. . ." He stops as the old drawbridge with a great creaking starts to rise. "Hurrah! It's working. Good old Rollo!" cries Bingo. Up it goes, but at the very moment it shuts off the castle gate Rollo appears at a window. "They've escaped," he shouts. "They're trying to catch me. I'll have to jump!"

Before the others can say anything Rollo climbs onto the window ledge. "Here goes!" he calls out as he stands poised with his hands above his head. "Is he a good swimmer?" breathes Bingo. "Yes, but I just hope the moat's deep enough," Rupert says. Then Rollo plunges. He barely makes a splash as he hits the water. The others hold their breath. Then Rollo's laughing head pops up near the bank. Bingo and Rupert let out great sighs of relief as the gipsy boy swims to the side.

RUPERT AND BINGO FIND A ROPE

"It's lucky you can swim so well.
You had us worried, truth to tell."

The two pals find a length of rope.
There's something on the end, they hope.

They pull a net up to the brink.
It looks like robbers' loot, they think.

"The drawbridge was their hiding place.
Here's P.C. Growler to give chase!"

"It's a jolly good thing you can dive and swim so well," laughs Rupert as he helps Rollo out of the water. "I told you I could look after myself, didn't I?" grins the boy. Suddenly Rupert has a thought. "But if you could raise the drawbridge surely the men will be able to lower it again." "Not without a lot of trouble," Rollo says. "I jammed the lifting machinery before I left." The gipsy boy is wringing out his clothes when Bingo and Rupert notice a rope at the edge of the moat.

"What do you make of this, Rollo?" they call. The boy examines the rope. "I think it was put there for a reason," he says. "We didn't see it before because it was hidden by the drawbridge. Let's see what's on the end of it." The three chums grab the rope and haul hard on it. At last a big net filled with packages emerges from the water. "I say, that drawbridge was being used as a hiding place!" gasps Rupert. Just then the Squire and P.C. Growler turn up on the motorcycle.

RUPERT POSES A PROBLEM

"They are the thieves, we've proof enough,
With their sack full of stolen stuff."

Says Growler, "First, I'll summon aid."
A walkie-talkie call is made.

"The drawbridge jammed? To cross the moat
The police will have to use a boat."

The Squire comes forward: "No they won't.
I know a way that most folk don't."

The Squire and the village policeman can hardly believe their ears as they hear how Rollo kept the robbers trapped by raising the drawbridge. "That was a plucky thing to do," declares the Squire as the chums finish the story. Next P.C. Growler is shown the sack full of the Squire's valuables. He says, "Enough proof here. I'm sure these are the pair of villains we've been after for some time." Before Rupert and his chums can tell about their find in the moat P.C. Growler takes out his walkie-talkie and asks for more policemen to be sent to the castle. "But how are they going to get into the castle?" Rupert asks. "The drawbridge is up and Rollo has jammed the machinery so that no one can lower it." "Oh dear!" says P.C. Growler. "I didn't think of that." But the Squire has the answer. "I've made a study of this castle," he says. "I know all the ins and outs. Now if you'll just follow me I'll show you something in those bushes very few people know about."

RUPERT SEES A SECRET WAY

A secret way, the old Squire shows,
That deep into the castle goes.

"More stolen goods! All proof enough
They used the moat to hide the stuff."

"You well may frown," the policeman yells.
"You'll soon be locked up tight in cells!"

"Well done, Bingo! I must say
Your clever gadget saved the day!"

The chums and P.C. Growler follow the Squire into the bushes where the old gentleman stops beside a square stone set into the ground. With the help of the policeman he raises the slab to reveal a hole below. "It's a secret passage!" Bingo gasps. "Yes," says the Squire, "it leads under the moat to a hidden door in the castle vaults. The police can easily get in this way." Much happier, P.C. Growler allows the chums to lead him back to the moat where they open the net and unwrap all the packages. "More stolen property!" exclaims P.C. Growler. Then he looks up and sees the two men at a window. "You'll soon be under arrest!" he calls sternly. Then while he waits for the other police to arrive he hears the full story from the Squire and the chums. "So you see Bingo's invention was really useful," Rupert laughs. P.C. Growler pats Bingo's shoulder. "Always said that you'd invent something really worthwhile. Credit to Nutwood, that's what you are, young Bingo!" he says.

RUPERT and the
WICKED UNCLE

Telling of Rupert's meeting with some of the people from his story-book and of an exciting chase.

RUPERT BEGINS TO WONDER

*Here's Rupert lying down to look
At his enormous picture book.*

*His Mummy says, "Just come with me!
These pictures all alive you'll see."*

*"Please tell me, Daddy," Rupert cries,
"Whatever is this big surprise?"*

*Soon by the wall he stands to stare
At all his picture people there.*

Rupert is quietly reading his favourite picture-book when his mother comes in. "I say, Mummy," he calls, "I do wish all the people I've been reading about were real and not just stories. There's the Old Woman in a Shoe and Aladdin and Babes in the Wood and . . ." Mrs. Bear laughs and interrupts him. "They are real sometimes," she says. "In fact Daddy and I are going to show you some of them this afternoon, so run and get washed and put your coat on."

As they walk down the high street Rupert begs his Daddy to tell him where they are going, but Mr. Bear only smiles. "Be patient and wait till we get there," he says, "then you'll find out the surprise we've prepared for you." As they approach the shops Rupert lags behind. "Why, just look here!" he cries, "there are great big pictures of the people in my book." "Yes, most of them are in other towns," says Mr. Bear mysteriously, "but come on, you mustn't dawdle or we shall be late for the opening."

RUPERT GETS A SIGNAL

"What is it all about," says he,
"This puzzle is too hard for me!"

At last they walk in through a door,
And Rupert wonders more and more.

Then Rupert quickly turns to find
A little boy is there behind.

"He's run away! Where has he gone?"
Cries Rupert, as he follows on.

Rupert can't yet understand what is happening but he runs to join the others and before long they are walking up some wide steps towards a gorgeous building and past some pictures of the Babes in the Wood. "Is this a Palace?" whispers the little bear as a tall man in a bright uniform shows them along a corridor and into a tiny room which has one wall missing. Rupert finds himself gazing into a huge space crowded with people. Some just below him are playing all sorts of musical instruments.

Rupert wants to ask all sorts of questions but Mrs. Bear makes him keep quiet. "This is a theatre and we are going to see a pantomime, so you must not talk too loudly," she says. All at once a slight noise makes Rupert turn. The door behind him has opened and a small boy is peeping at him. The boy beckons urgently and then disappears. "What does he want?" thinks Rupert as he grabs his scarf and follows. "And where has he gone? This long corridor seems to be empty."

Rupert and the Wicked Uncle

RUPERT MEETS THE BABES

*"Dear me!" he says, "now what are these?
They look to me like cardboard trees."*

*"Now these look more like real trees should,
With fresh green leaves, and trunks of wood."*

*At last he looks, and cries with joy,
"Ah, there you are, my little boy."*

*The boy says, "Oh, our feet are sore!
We cannot wander any more."*

Rupert goes down the steps. "That boy must have gone this way," he mutters, "but this is a queer place. The trees and the mushrooms seem to be the right shape but they're all made of cloth or cardboard." He gazes around and wonders if he ought to return to his parents. Then he decides to explore a bit farther. "This is getting queerer and queerer," he says. "Only half the trees are made of cardboard now, the others are growing. I do believe I'm going into a real wood."

The wood gets lighter still and ahead of him Rupert hears voices. In a clearing he sees the little figure whom he has been following. The boy is trying to comfort a still smaller girl who is crying. "So here you are at last," cries Rupert. "Who are you, and why did you beckon me?" "Don't you know us?" says the boy. "We're the Babes in the Wood and we need help. We're trying to escape from our Wicked Uncle. We've run and run and now my little sister is almost too tired to go any farther."

RUPERT GIVES A WARNING

"But look! Our wicked Uncle's here!
We must run fast! Come on, my dear!"

"Here is the wood. Let's run inside,
And see if we can safely hide."

"Hooray!" they cry, "our lives we'll save
If once we're safe inside this cave."

"But wait," says Rupert, "just look here
At these fresh footsteps, plain and clear."

Rupert is very worried at what he has heard. "You'd both better rest a bit," he says. "It seems sheltered and safe here." As he speaks a distant shout reaches their ears and the boy turns sharply to peer around a bush. "There he is, it's our Wicked Uncle. He's spotted us!" he gasps. He grabs his sister's hand and off they go again. "We must keep in the shelter of the trees and hide if we can," says Rupert as they reach a part of the wood where there are lots of great boulders and the bushes are thick.

The three friends run out of the wood and find themselves at the foot of a rocky hillside. "Oh dear, I'm too tired to climb that," sobs the little girl. "There's no need," declares the boy. "Look, here's the entrance to a fine cave. It's quite dark and Uncle would never be able to see us." They go inside but Rupert pauses and gazes at the ground. "Hi, come back," he calls, "you may find more trouble in there. D'you see these marks on the ground? Somebody else has passed this way not long ago."

RUPERT PLANS TO HIDE

"Hide in these jars," he cries, "for, see,
There's two for you, and one for me."

They do not wait for any more,
But jump inside, amongst the straw.

Then Rupert hears feet running fast
And sees their Uncle hurry past.

Then men pick up the jars and go
Into the cavern dark and low.

At Rupert's call the others return and look anxiously at the foot-marks. While they pause they hear muffled voices from far inside the cave. "Oh dear, we're trapped!" whispers the little girl. "Somebody in there has heard us. We daren't go in. We can't stop here or our Wicked Uncle will catch us." Rupert gazes around quickly. "Yes, we *can* stay here," he says. "See, there are some big jars filled with loose straw. Can't we get in and hide?" "Grand idea!" cries the boy.

Hardly are the little people in the jars than foot steps are heard rushing along. Peeping out cautiously Rupert sees that the Wicked Uncle has gone past and is running furiously down the farther slope. A large man strides from the cave and gazes fiercely around. Then he claps his hands sharply and two others run to him. He gives an order in a low voice and they all move toward the jars, tip them sideways and, hoisting them on to their backs, march into the rocky cave.

RUPERT GETS A RIDE

The men say voices they have heard,
(The little friends say not a word.)

The jars are lowered by the men,
And Rupert sees them go again.

He listens. As the last sound stops,
Out of the jar his head he pops.

"They've gone!" he cries, "come out! All clear!
Let's try to get away from here."

The three men carry their burdens carefully through many passages. "I heard voices outside," says the leader gruffly. "There was a grown man running. I liked him not. We must hide these jars of ours, they are valuable to us." They lower the jars gently at the end of an inner passage. "Yea, I, too, heard voices, but they were young voices," says one. "There is mystery here. Where are they now?" As they move away Rupert again peeps very cautiously out of the straw.

When the men have gone Rupert screws up his courage, gets out as quietly as he can, and tiptoes around the end of the passage. "This must be a magic cave," he thinks. "Why is it so light. It ought to be pitch dark." Then he returns to the other jars and calls gently. The Babes in the Wood have been very frightened but at the sound of his voice they, too, climb out. "We're all right so far," whispers Rupert. "We'd better leave the jars and hide in the rocks."

RUPERT FINDS THE TREASURE

"This really is the queerest sight,
With passages to left and right."

He finds a cave. "Oh, look!" he cries,
"I really can't believe my eyes."

There's silver, gold and jewels rare
Among the wondrous treasure there.

The little girl cries, "See this ring!
It really is the strangest thing."

The little girl is too frightened to go back in the direction that the men have taken. "Well, let's see if there is any other way out," suggests Rupert. After a while the boy stops. "This is a weird place," he whispers, "I don't like it. Let's go back to the jars." But Rupert begs them to explore one more passage and he leads the way. The passage ends in a small cave which he enters. Then he pauses suddenly. "Come here quickly," he calls, "just see what I've found."

At the sound of excitement in Rupert's voice the others hurry to him. "What is it?" demands the boy. "Look, gold and silks and jewels!" cries the little bear. "There must be a huge treasure here." But the girl is already rummaging amongst the pretty things that are strewn around. "Here's a queer ring," she says. "It's too big for a finger and too small for a bracelet. I wonder if it's real gold. It's a strange colour." "Do you like it?" says Rupert. "Then let me polish it up for you and see."

RUPERT MEETS THE GENIE

"Yes, such a ring I've never seen,"
Says Rupert, "look! I'll rub it clean."

The genie cries, "Whate'er you say,
I am your slave, and must obey."

"Twice you may ask, and then no more."
The three friends stand and gaze with awe.

The cavern cracks, and with a shout,
The Babes and Rupert all run out.

Rupert takes his handkerchief and gives the ring a vigorous rub. There is a flash and a cloud of smoke and from it surges the head and shoulders of a huge figure. The Babes in the Wood are terrified and scurry behind a rock but Rupert stands his ground and, after the first shock of surprise, his expression changes. "Why, I know who this is," he cries. "He's in my story-book at home. He's a genie!" "'Tis true, little master," says the genie in a deep voice. "The ring you hold makes me your slave."

Rupert thinks quickly. "Oh, there are lots of things we would like you to do," he says. "Nay, little master," replies the genie, "the ring is old and now only gives two wishes to the one who holds it. So consider carefully before you speak." "Well," murmurs Rupert, "what we really need first is to find a short cut from this cave out into the open air." "So be it," booms the great figure. "Behold, 'tis done." He waves his arms and with a noise like thunder the wall of rock splits from top to bottom.

RUPERT'S SECOND REQUEST

Hemmed in by rocks so big and tall,
They cannot scramble out at all.

They say, "Our last wish we must try."
The genie answers, "Here am I."

The magic words have just been said,
The ring flies over Rupert's head.

And then they see a smiling sprite,
And stand and stare at this strange sight.

No sooner are the little friends in the open air than the cleft behind them closes with another mighty bang. "Whew! We're well out of that," says Rupert. They seem to have reached a rocky gorge filled with enormous boulders that have fallen from the cliffs above. "This is as bad as ever," says the boy, "my sister would never have the strength to climb out of this." "Nor should I," sighs Rupert, "but I've one wish left. Let's try again." He rubs the ring and once more the genie appears.

"Thank goodness you've come," says Rupert. "This place is as bad as the cave. Please show us the way to open country with fields and trees." As he speaks the ring flies out of his hand and is caught by the genie. "That is your last . wish, little master," says the voice. "After this I can serve you no longer. Farewell." With another flash the genie and the cloud of smoke vanish and in their place appears a cheeky little sprite smiling at them from a shelf of rock.

RUPERT LEARNS TO FLY

*"Just think you're flying, and you'll see
It's easy, but you must watch me."*

*So over those great rocks so high,
They spread their arms, and off they fly.*

*But as upon the grass they light,
They look, and see a dreadful sight.*

*"There is no time to lose," they cry
As o'er the trees they quickly fly.*

The sprite grins at the surprise on the faces of the three friends. "So you want to get out of the rocky gorge?" he says. "Nothing is simpler. You must fly." "But—how *can* we?" gasps Rupert. "Only do as I do," laughs the other. "Just think about flying and watch me." Rupert and the Babes do as he tells them. They spread their arms and find themselves soaring above the rocks into the open country. "There, that's grand," says the sprite as he alights.

As Rupert and the Babes come to earth the sprite gives a sudden cry of fright and takes off again. "What's the matter with him?" says the girl. But Rupert points. "It's your Wicked Uncle," he cries. "Quick, there's no time to lose." Fixing their eyes on the sprite they spread their arms and are in the air before he reaches them. "I say, that was a near thing!" gasps the boy. "Hi, look at that great shoe down there," interrupts Rupert. "That's the shoe the Old Woman lives in with her children."

RUPERT CONFOUNDS THE UNCLE

A Shoe they see as down they look
Just like the one in Rupert's book.

The children all run up and say
"We are so glad you've come to play."

They all run round the Shoe so fast,
The Uncle gives it up at last.

"They've beaten me," he sighs aloud,
I'll never find them in that crowd."

Rupert and the Babes find to their dismay that their power to fly has gone and they glide downwards. The Old Woman who lives in a Shoe spies them coming. "Look, we have visitors, they must be special ones for they come by air," she calls. "We must make them welcome." Her children run towards the strangers as they alight. "Oh, how lovely: Have you come to play with us?" they cry. "What are your names? Where are you from? How did you manage to fly? Have you had tea?"

The Wicked Uncle has seen what has happened and he approaches quickly just as dozens of children are welcoming the new arrivals. Rupert sees him and warns them, but the children laugh merrily and, taking the Babes with them, they run round and round the Shoe. The Uncle chases them furiously until he gets giddy. Then he throws down his cudgel in disgust. "Tchah, foiled again!" he growls angrily. "I could never pick them out of that crowd." And he strides away frowning.

RUPERT WAVES GOOD-BYE

The children laugh and shout with glee,
And then run in to make the tea.

The Woman asks, "Why not stay here?"
But Rupert says, "Not me, I fear."

"And as I can no longer fly,
Home through the woods I'll walk. Good-bye!"

"Why, this is very strange," cries he,
"I'm sure I've seen this cardboard tree!"

Some of the children go into the Shoe to make tea while the others dance round their new friends and sing. Then the three pals tell of their strange journey and the Old Woman calls them to her. "I've had a lovely idea," she says. "It's ages since we had any new children here. If you go away now that Wicked Uncle will be sure to catch you. Why don't you join us and live here always?" The Babes in the Wood are overjoyed and cling to her, but Rupert pauses and looks thoughtful.

Rupert quickly makes up his mind. "It's very, very kind of you," he says, "but my Mummy might not like it." Then he stops. "Oh dear," he moans, "how *can* I get back. Without the sprite I can't fly and . . ." "Don't worry, it's quite easy," says the Old Woman. "Just make for the nearest bit of woodland and keep straight on. So she and the Babes wave good-bye and he is soon on his way. After a few minutes he gazes round in astonishment. "Surely I've been here before!" he mutters.

Back up the steps he climbs, and there
He finds the passage, quiet and bare.

And in the box, three empty chairs!
Poor little Rupert stands and stares.

"Oh dear," he cries, "they've gone away!
No, here they are again! Hooray!"

His Mummie cries, "You've missed the show,"
But Rupert smiles and says, "Oh no!"

Rupert is right. The real trees and bushes have been left behind and he is back among the cloth and cardboard scenery. "Well, this is fine," he says, "but how I got here I can't imagine." He opens the door to rejoin Mr. and Mrs. Bear and then stops. The chairs are empty and there is nobody in sight. "Gracious what can have happened?" he thinks. "The show must be over and everybody gone home." Feeling anxious he runs on down the corridor.

To his great relief Rupert meets his parents almost at once. "Where *have* you been? We've been terribly worried," says Mr. Bear. "Thank goodness you're safe!" adds Mrs. Bear. "To think that you missed seeing the Babes in the Wood! What a pity." "Missed them?" cries Rupert. "I didn't miss anything. I was with them all the time. Didn't you see me? Let's hurry home. Then I'll show you my picture-book and tell you everything that I've been doing."

RUPERT and the
BUZZING BOX

How Rupert and Bill earn
a ride in a motorboat and
win a medal.

RUPERT GETS AN INVITATION

Bill Badger's uncle writes to say,
"May Bill and Rupert come to stay?"

So Rupert asks kind Mrs. Bear,
Who says, "All right; but do take care."

In great excitement off they run,
Quite certain they'll have lots of fun.

The rabbit twins are sailing by,
And turn in answer to their cry.

Bill Badger has received a letter from his uncle asking him to come up to his riverside home and stay awhile. Bill packs a rucksack and at once rushes up to Rupert's cottage to ask Mrs. Bear if Rupert can go along with him. Mrs. Bear looks rather doubtful, but Bill pleads so hard that she smiles and says, "Oh! all right, off you go, but do be careful, you seem to get in such adventures these days."

Promising to take great care of each other the two pals set off on their journey. "We'd better get a move on," says Bill. "It's much farther than you would imagine when you follow the river bank with all its twists and turns." Steadily they plod on when suddenly along comes a sailing-boat with the Rabbit twins at the tiller. "I do wish we had a boat, don't you, Rupert?" says Bill. "Well, we haven't," says the little bear, "but we may get the next best thing, which is a lift in the twins' boat, so shout and attract their attention."

RUPERT ASKS FOR A LIFT

They steer their sailing-boat with care,
And come close to the little bear.

"We'd like a lift," is Rupert's plea,
"Of course! Jump in," the twins agree.

They sail along at such a rate,
The chums are sure they won't be late.

An island they've not seen before,
Makes Rupert eager to explore.

The Rabbit twins steer their boat very cleverly and soon they are running smoothly alongside the river bank while Rupert shouts and explains that he and Bill have a long way to go up the river and please could they have a lift. The sailors are only too glad to be able to do their pals a good turn and quickly work their boat to the shore so that going aboard is quite an easy matter.

The boat is soon under way again and glides along at such a speed that the pals realize they will have no need to worry about reaching Bill's uncle in plenty of time. They lean over the side and call a cheery greeting to Mrs. Duck who is out with her triplets for their daily swimming lesson. Soon, in the distance, they see an island right in the centre of the river, and excitely all four start to wonder if it is occupied. Rupert, now that he is sure that they have plenty of time, begs the Rabbit twins to steer the boat near enough to see if there is a landing place, for he would like to have a peep round.

RUPERT IS TRICKED

The Rabbit twins agree to land,
And they run their boat on to the sand.

The twins say they will stay just there,
And wait for Bill and Rupert Bear.

But when the chums are out of sight,
The rabbits leave them to their plight.

Now Bill and Rupert think it's fun,
Not knowing what the twins have done.

They soon find a lovely sandy strip on which they make a perfect landing and quickly reefing sail all four step ashore. Rupert and Bill take their rucksacks and invite the twins to share the lunch they have brought with them. "No thank you," they say. "You go ahead and we'll wait for you— we must not leave our boat unattended." So Rupert and Bill go on alone and, finding some old, very worn steps, they start to climb.

As soon as they are well on their way the Rabbit twins put their heads together and plan to play a trick on the pals by sailing off and leaving them stranded. Still steadily climbing, Rupert and Bill are so excited that they take no notice of the little bird who is trying to warn them of the trick the twins are playing. Before long they reach the end of their climb and there, in the distance, across the island is a ruin of what must have been a lovely old castle. "Let's go and examine it," says Bill. "I'm sure the twins will wait for us."

RUPERT FINDS A BOX

A ruined castle now they've found,
They simply have to look around.

"Look at this earth," cries Rupert Bear,
"I wonder who's been digging there?"

The chums go wandering about,
Till Rupert gives a sudden shout.

"Look what I've found!" he cries with glee,
"It's worth a lot, its seems to me."

Still not suspecting the Rabbit twins Rupert and Bill press on until they reach the old ruins and, with their usual curiosity, they start to explore. "It's very odd," says Bill. "I don't think anybody can possibly live here." The little bear turns round. "Perhaps not," he says, "but somebody is here or has been here. Just look at this new ladder and this spade; it's not long since that was used." They carefully search the digging grounds but become more and more puzzled as they fail to unearth a single clue to show what the previous visitors were looking for.

Soon the pals decide to examine the other parts of the old ruin and Bill comes running when he hears an excited shout. "Whatever is it, Rupert?" asks Bill, when he sees Rupert holding a metal box. "I'm not sure," replies the little bear, "but it looks very valuable. It must have been left by the people who have been digging here; anyway we'd better take it with us."

RUPERT PRESSES THE SWITCH

They really must be getting back,
But now they cannot find the track.

The chums walk round as in a maze,
Then think they will go different ways.

This seems to be the wisest plan,
To each discover what he can.

They walk in circles as before,
And meet right at the start once more.

"What on earth shall we do now?" asks Bill. "I don't see the track we came in by." Rupert looks around but is in no way upset. "Why worry?" he asks. "There must be dozens of ways to that little bay where we landed." So, away they go, but it is not long before both Rupert and Bill realize that they are really lost and have only been going round and round in circles. "The only thing we can do," says Rupert, "is to split up. You go one way and I'll go the other and as soon as we find the path to the beach we must yell out and stay where we are until the other one, guided by the calls, joins him."

This is agreed upon and so Bill waves good-bye and sets off in the opposite direction to that taken by Rupert. Unfortunately, once again they walk in a circle and it is not long before Bill comes through some trees to find Rupert standing there and fiddling about with a switch he has found on the metal box that he picked up in the ruins.

RUPERT MARKS THE SPOT

"Well," Rupert cries, "this box is queer;
Strange clicks and buzzing sounds I hear."

When Rupert starts to move around,
The strange box makes a louder sound.

One place is very loud indeed,
The buzzing comes at greater speed.

The chums decide to mark the spot,
With all the paper they have got.

As Bill approaches, Rupert puts the metal box to his ear and listens. "Whatever is the matter, Rupert?" asks Bill. "You look terribly excited." The little bear explains to Bill that he first pressed the switch by accident and found that the box made a buzzing sound whenever he stood in a certain place. "You see, Bill," he says, "when I stand here the buzzing is very faint, but as I walk over here it gets louder and louder until I get here and then the box nearly jumps out of my hand." "It must be jolly important," says Bill. "What are we going to do now?"

"I tell you what," says Rupert, "we will mark the spot with a stick and a paper bag and then we will tear up the rest of the paper that we have and lay a trail." "That's a good idea," says Bill, "and we will make for the ruins and start from there." Quickly the two pals get to work and before long they have enough paper to lay the trail for as good a paper-chase as they have ever taken part in.

Now Rupert lays the trail all right,
And soon the ruins are in sight.

Some men have now returned to find,
The box that they had left behind.

Another man soon finds the pair,
And asks them what they're doing there.

The master comes to see them and
Soon spies the box in Rupert's hand.

Away the pals run, with Rupert dropping a paper trail as he follows Bill still clutching his surprise metal box. Although they seem to have been wandering around the island for ages it is not long before they arrive back at the ruins. They are just about to rush in when they hear voices, and Rupert peers round a stone pillar to hear an old gentleman saying to his comrades, "But I tell you it must be here, and what is more it must be found, for we cannot go on with our search without it."

The little bear turns to tell Bill what he has heard when a smiling-faced young fellow pops round the corner and says, "Hi! you two, what are you doing here? Just you come along with me and see my master." Quickly the two little pals are led to the old gentleman who appears to be the leader, but before their captor can say a word the leader catches sight of the black box and such questions as, "How did you find it? Where did you find it?" and "Why did you take it away?" come tumbling from his lips.

RUPERT LEADS THE WAY

The little bear tells how he found,
Their precious box upon the ground.

The box is used to help them trace,
Rare metals buried in a place.

This news makes Rupert shout with glee,
"I think we found some; come with me!"

The paper trail is very plain,
And soon they reach that place again.

When he finds that the men are by no means cross with them, Rupert at once hands the metal box to the leader, explaining exactly where they found it and that they only carried it about with them for fear that someone might steal it. The old man is so delighted that he shows Rupert and Bill how to work the machine which, he says, he is using to help in his search for rare metals.

When Rupert hears this he dances with excitement and explains to the leader how they got lost and, when he accidentally touched the switch, the box began to make a buzzing sound. On hearing the news the old gentleman and his helpers are overjoyed and ask the pals if it is possible to take them to the place. With happy grins Rupert and Bill explain how they marked the spot and laid the trail. Soon all the party are on their way, and it is not long before Rupert is pointing out the paper bag on top of the stick just where he has left it.

RUPERT GETS A REWARD

Now eagerly they gather round,
To listen for the tell-tale sound.

The master gives a joyful shout,
"This is the place without a doubt!"

Then greatly to the chums' surprise,
"These medals are for you," he cries.

It's getting rather late, and so
To find the Rabbit twins they go.

As soon as they are all collected round the paper bag on the stick the old gentleman takes the metal box and, pressing the switch, works the machine in the same way that he had demonstrated to Rupert and Bill. Very soon he has proof of the accuracy of Rupert's story for, as he moves, the box buzzes louder and louder and soon he is flinging his arms in the air and shouting his joy to the skies. "This is the place, without a doubt," he yells "now we can really get to work."

When he has calmed down a little, the leader of the party produces a medal each for Rupert and Bill as a reward for great help and at the same time asks if there is anything he can do for them. "Yes, please!" says Rupert. "We want to get down to the sandy beach where the Rabbit twins left us, and we cannot find our way." The old man chuckles. "Ho! Ho! that's very easy," says he. Hoisting Rupert on his shoulder and clasping Bill firmly by the hand the party set off to find the boat.

RUPERT CALLS FOR HELP

They find the sandy beach all right,
But there's no sailing-boat in sight.

Now Rupert feels there's something wrong,
To keep the twins away so long.

He tells the man what has occurred,
Then off they go without a word.

He takes them to the river, where
A motor-boat is waiting there.

Before long the old man and his helpers have found the sandy landing beach, and after many expressions of renewed thanks they turn and go back to their work on the island. Rupert and Bill, however, are much troubled because there is no sign of their boat. "I'll bet they've played a trick and gone off and left us," says Bill, but Rupert doesn't think so. "It's not like them," he says. "They are good pals and have such kind natures—no, I think something has happened to them."

Without wasting any more time they return and explain to the old man that their boat has gone and that they cannot go on their journey. The old gentleman only smiles. "You come with me, I think I can surprise you." Soon they come to a lovely powerful-looking motor-boat with more men of the party standing guard. over it. The leader orders them to take Rupert and Bill up the river and drop them right at the front door of the cottage belonging to Bill's uncle.

RUPERT AND BILL ARRIVE

The twins are sitting on their boat,
Which is capsized, but still afloat.

They have not come to any harm,
Although it filled them with alarm.

The chums soon find it's time to land,
Their journey's end is near at hand.

Bill's uncle's glad that they could come,
And welcomes Rupert and his chum.

Rupert stands on the bows of the motor-boat as it races up the river. Suddenly he gives a shout for he has spied the Rabbit twins sitting on top of their overturned boat. Soon the shivering pair are being lifted to safety. "Oh, Rupert," they say, "we really are sorry for playing such a silly prank. We decided to come back for you almost at once, but a gust of wind caught us unawares and the boat capsized." "We didn't think you'd really abandon us," Rupert tells the twins and that cheers them up.

On such a fast boat the journey to the riverside home of Bill's uncle takes only a short time and soon the two pals are standing on a landing-stage waving their goodbyes. When the boat has vanished round a bend in the river Rupert and Bill continue their journey on foot. Before long they are telling of their adventures and proudly displaying their medals to Bill's uncle who has come to the door of his cottage to welcome them. "You two certainly do have some adventures," he chuckles.

Rupert's Memory Test

Don't try this memory test until you have read all the stories in the book. Once you have read them study the pictures on this page. Each of them is from a picture you will have seen in one or other of the stories. Then try to answer the questions about them at the bottom of the page. When you are done check the stories to see if you were right.

AND NOW DO YOU KNOW...

1. What is happening in the village shop?
2. What does the bag on the stick show?
3. What has the little girl found?
4. What does Bingo find for Mr. Bear?
5. Why is Algy floating in the air?
6. Who is coming down this ladder?
7. A pill like this can lift what?
8. What are the Rabbit twins plotting?
9. What is on the end of this rope?
10. What does the man want for his puzzle?
11. What pantomime is Rupert going to see?
12. Why is Algy hanging on to Rupert?
13. How does Rupert use these jars?
14. What are Rupert and Rollo reading?
15. Why was the dog taught not to bark?
16. What does Rupert see in the sky?

*"Go and ask Algy if you are
To go by train or in their car."*

*Thinks Rupert, gazing at the sky,
"What is that curious thing I spy?"*

Such excitement in the Bear house. The family is getting ready to go on holiday. Rupert who is always excited before a holiday is looking forward to this one even more than usual. For not only are they going to one of his most favourite places —Sandy Bay—but one of his pals, Algy Pug, is going there, too, with his Mummy. Suddenly Mrs. Bear looks up from her packing. "My memory!" she exclaims. "Mrs. Pug suggested you and Algy might travel together, but I can't remember if you're to go in their car or if Algy's coming with us by train. Still, there's time for you to go to their house and ask." "If I'm to go by car need I come back and tell you?" asks Rupert. Mrs. Bear thinks. "No," she says. "If you're not back at once I'll know you're going with them." So Rupert sets out for Algy's house but as he trots along suddenly he notices something strange in the sky.

he Wrong Sweets

Algy makes a bad mistake about some "sweets" he finds. And the result is high adventure for both Rupert and him.

*"Look at those boxes in the sky!
And paper bags! I wonder why."*

*More flying boxes Rupert sees,
Floating up from 'midst the trees.*

Rupert stops to watch the curious object in the sky until it drifts gently out of sight. But then to his astonishment another one appears, and another and another. Rupert scratches his head. "Why, they're just little boxes and paper bags," he murmurs to himself. "But what on earth are they doing up there? What's keeping them up?" He goes on watching the bags and boxes. "I'd understand it if there was a very strong wind blowing, but there isn't." Then he thinks, "I wonder who they belong to." After a while he notices that all the bags and boxes seem to be coming from one place—a stretch of woodland beyond a fence. Every now and then a box or a bag pops up from the trees and goes drifting up into the blue. Rupert is so very curious that he forgets he's in a hurry. "I must find out what this is all about," he thinks and scrambles through the fence.

RUPERT MEETS HIS CHUM

"Here comes a heavy wooden crate.
It floats as if it had no weight!"

As Rupert hurries on he spies
Algy himself. "Hello!" he cries.

"My Mummy says that I may come
By train with you!" exclaims his chum.

"I was just going to find out
What all those boxes are about."

Just before he reaches the wood Rupert stops and stares. Up from the trees comes floating a much bigger thing than the boxes and bags he has seen so far. "It's a wooden crate!" he gasps in astonishment. "It must be heavy yet it's floating up there as if it has no weight at all!" He is just about to carry on and find where the things are coming from when he remembers his errand. He turns in the direction of Mrs. Pug's cottage and at that moment he hears his name called and, to his surprise,

Algy himself appears from the wood. "Hey, I'm on my way to your house," he shouts. "And I'm on my way to your home to see if I am travelling in your car," laughs the little bear. Algy chuckles, "What a lark! My Mummy says I may go by train with you. I came through the wood for a change. What a bit of luck we met. But what are you doing in the wood?" "I saw some strange things in the air and I was going to try to find where they came from," Rupert replies.

RUPERT TRIES A "SWEET"

"Do try a sweet. They're some new kind,
But haven't got much taste, you'll find."

"Not too bad—not as nice as chocs—
Oh, look! Here comes another box!"

"Whose are they?" Algy turns to gaze.
"Let's have a search and see," he says.

But Rupert says. "No time to waste.
We'd miss our train. We must make haste."

"We better get back to my house," says Rupert. "But let's keep a look-out for any more of those strange flying things." "Right," Algy says. "But before we start have some of these. I've lots more." And he holds out a handful of what look like sweets. "Are they acid drops?" Rupert asks. "Well, no . . . in fact they haven't much taste at all," says Algy. "Try one." Rupert takes out one of the sweets he has put in his pocket and pops it into his mouth. "Not too bad . . ." he starts to say. Then he stops and points. "Another flying box!" he exclaims. "It's a cardboard box," Algy gasps. "How is it staying up there?" Now Rupert tells him about all the other boxes and bags he has seen floating up out of the trees. "But why didn't I see anything when I came through the wood?" Algy wants to know. "Let's go back now and take a look." Rupert hesitates, but then he says, "No, we'd better get back to my house as soon as we can. Remember we've a train to catch."

RUPERT IS DISMAYED

*"Just for the journey, for a treat,
I'll get more of these sweets to eat."*

"Not yours? You found *them on that tray?"
Cries Rupert, staring in dismay.*

*"You mustn't eat strange sweets, you know!
Didn't your Mummy tell you so?"*

*"Perhaps the owner can be found.
Let's see if anyone's around."*

But still Algy hangs back. "What is it now?" asks Rupert. "Oh, I just thought we might as well have some more of those sweets for the journey," his pal replies. Rupert is puzzled. "Why, where did you get them?" he says. "Is there a shop in the wood?" "No, I didn't *buy* them," replies Algy. "I found them . . . Look! There they are!" And he points to a tray full of them on a nearby tree stump. Rupert stares in dismay. "But they're not yours at all, Algy. You shouldn't have touched them!" The more he thinks about what his pal has done, the more horrified Rupert becomes. "Surely your Mummy must have told you never to eat sweets unless you know where they've come from . . . and, oh dear, we don't even know if they are sweets." All at once Algy looks very unhappy. "A-and I've just eaten two!" he quavers. "Well, I'm going to take this tray and see if it belongs to anyone," Rupert says, making up his mind. "Then we must hurry home because we might be taken ill."

RUPERT MEETS THE INVENTOR

"We might take ill, so I'll go on,"
Says Algy Pug, and then he's gone.

Thinks Rupert, "I shall ask that man.
"I'm sure he'll help me if he can."

"Yes, mine. But they're not sweets at all,
And powerful though they're very small."

"They're my invention and they've done
Great things but I've not tasted one."

But by this time Algy is really frightened and won't go with Rupert to search for the owner of the tray. "I'll just walk slowly towards your cottage," he says in a little voice. "You can catch me up." So the little bear pushes on into the wood alone. After a while he hears noises and starts towards them. Suddenly there is a clearing ahead and in it a car, a tent and a man who seems to be doing something with a small stove. "I'll go and ask him if he knows anything about these

sweets." Rupert thinks. At the sound of Rupert's approach the stranger gives a start. "Oh, please, are these your sweets?" the little bear asks him. The man stares then chuckles, "They're mine, but they're not sweets, oh no!" "Oh dear," Rupert says shakily, "are they poison?" "Don't know," the man says. "Never tasted one." Surprisingly he seems amused. "They're a new invention of mine and I'm hoping that one day soon they may astonish the world," he goes on.

"They make those heavy boxes light,
And might help wingless folk take flight."

"One small one," Rupert is informed,
"Will lift a heavy box, when warmed."

"I'll put in one small piece of 'sweet'
Then warm the box up in this heat."

Gently the box begins to rise
From Rupert's hands and off it flies.

Rupert is still very worried but the man seems to think that the little bear's serious face means he is interested in the invention. He goes on, "Some day my invention may make airplanes weigh next to nothing. It might even let men fly without using airplanes at all!" "And you were trying it out with those bags and boxes?" exclaims Rupert who really is interested now despite his fears. The stranger nods. "One of those 'sweets' as you call them, will, when it is warmed, lift a very heavy box. It needs only a tiny bit to lift a paper bag or a small box." Then the man goes on to explain that he left the tray of "sweets" on a tree stump because it was cool there. "It's such a hot day that I was afraid they might get too warm and turn into gas. Let me show you," he adds. He puts a very small piece of 'sweet' into a little box and holds it in the heat from his stove. Then after a few moments he hands it to Rupert. At once the box rises from his hands and floats away.

RUPERT TELLS ALGY

Rupert is scared of what's been done,
And dare not say he's eaten one.

"I must catch Algy up and tell
What's wrong. He's eaten two, as well."

"Those sweets have done me good. What fun!
Just see how I can jump and run!"

Then Rupert says, "I'll tell you why!
They made those bags and boxes fly!"

Rupert watches fascinated as the box drifts off. The stranger is surprised to see that the little bear looks more solemn than ever and doesn't seem excited by what he has seen. "Perhaps you'd like to try a bigger box, my young friend," he offers. But as he thinks about what he has seen a small piece of "sweet" do, Rupert becomes more and more dismayed. "Er, no thank you," he stammers. "I really must go after my pal." And he takes to his heels thinking, "Algy must be told about those wretched 'sweets' at once."

As he hurries toward Nutwood he spies his pal and calls to him. Algy turns. But now he looks quite cheerful: "I don't know what those things were I ate but I really feel extremely well. I can run and jump so easily now." "Yes, and I know why," pants Rupert. And all the cheerfulness fades from Algy's face as he hears Rupert's tale of his meeting with the man who invented the "sweets". "And I've swallowed two of them. Oh, what will happen to me?" he wails.

RUPERT'S CHUM TAKES OFF

*"The man who made them may know how
Those 'sweets' will act upon us now."*

*A cry makes Rupert turn around.
"Oh, help! My feet won't touch the ground!"*

*While Rupert tries to grab the pup,
Poor Algy just keeps floating up.*

*Rupert can only stand dismayed
While Algy's cries begin to fade.*

As Rupert tells how he watched a tiny piece of one of the 'sweets' send a box floating up into the air, Algy becomes more and more alarmed. "We're going back to see that inventor," Rupert decides. "There's no use standing here talking. That man made them and so he should know what we ought to do. Come on, let's hurry!" And the little bear sets off briskly with Algy following. Suddenly a cry makes him swing round. "Oh, Rupert, help me!" Algy shouts. "My feet won't stay on the ground!"

For a moment Rupert stares in astonishment as his chum seems to hover just above the grass. Then he runs back to him. But as he does so Algy starts to rise. He reaches out to try to catch hold of something but can't. "Stop playing about and come down at once!" cries Rupert. "I c-c-can't!" wails the pup. "Oh, please help!" But no matter how Rupert runs and jumps he can't reach his pal and he watches with horror as Algy floats gently away, up and up, his cries getting fainter.

RUPERT FOLLOWS HIS PAL

"Those 'sweets' got warm inside him, so
We might have known that up he'd go."

"I must get help!" He speeds along.
Then finds that something's badly wrong.

He floats up, tries to hold on and
The twig snaps clean off in his hand.

"Up here I can see such a way.
Is that the train to Sandy Bay?"

At first Rupert can't think what to do. For what seems a long time he just stands and watches Algy growing smaller and smaller as he drifts away over the countryside. Then he thinks, "It's those 'sweets'. The two he swallowed must have got warm inside him and now they're carrying him away like those bags and boxes. I must hurry and tell Dr. Lion or Constable Growler." He starts to run home to Nutwood thinking so much about poor Algy that at first he doesn't notice how long his strides are—almost like jumps. Then—horror!—all at once the grass seems to drop away from beneath his feet. "That 'sweet' that I ate!" he gasps. "It's working on me!" He grabs at a twig to try to stop himself from rising but it breaks off in his hand. Then he is high above the countryside and unable to do anything but turn slowly over and over as the breeze blows him away. "Oh dear," he thinks, "that's Nutwood station down there. And there's a train in. I hope it's not the Sandy Bay one."

RUPERT FLOATS OUT TO SEA

"Algy! But he can't hear me call.
Oh, dear, I hope that we don't fall."

And so he floats on helplessly,
Until at last he spies the sea.

He gazes down at beach and links.
"That could be Sandy Bay," he thinks

And now poor Rupert gets a fright.
He feels that he is losing height.

Rupert is surprised to find how quickly he stops being afraid of falling. He is still clutching the twig he snapped off when he tried to prevent himself from rising. As he floats above the little clouds he looks ahead and sees a small dot higher in the sky. "That must be Algy," he thinks "I don't suppose he'd hear me if I shouted. Even if he did, he wouldn't be able to turn back." And so Rupert goes drifting on, unable to do anything about it. Then far in the distance he catches sight of something blue and shining. "It's the sea," he says aloud. He floats steadily onwards to the coast. Seagulls wonder what the curious airborne object can be and come close to inspect him. "There's a big seaside place down there," he thinks. "I wonder if it's Sandy Bay. Can't tell from up here. Lots of people must be looking up at me. Probably think I'm a balloon." Then at the same moment he finds himself above the sea Rupert notices something. He's getting lower.

RUPERT MUST EAT A "SWEET"

He calls for help. His plight is grim.
A seagull comes to rescue him.

The helpful bird sees what is wrong,
And tows the little bear along.

The gull finds Rupert just too big.
It turns and—Oh! He's lost the twig!

"I've got some more sweets so I'll try
Just one to keep me floating high."

Down, down, down Rupert sinks towards the ocean. The waves that seemed so small when he was high up get bigger and bigger as he gets near them. What is happening is that the effect of the 'sweet' he ate is wearing off. "Oh, help!" he shouts as the waves get nearer and nearer. A few seagulls fly down to see what all the fuss is about and one of them squawks, "Hey, what are you doing flying? You're not a bird." "I can't explain now!" cries Rupert. "Please help me before I drop into the sea."

The big seagull seizes Rupert's twig in its beak and flaps slowly towards the shore. But the bird soon sees that it can't tow Rupert all the way to the shore. So it turns and makes for a bell-buoy where it hopes to land him. But as it does so the twig slips from Rupert's hand and once more he sinks towards the waves. Just when he has almost given up hope he remembers the rest of the 'sweets' in his pocket. "I've got to risk taking another," he thinks and feels for them.

RUPERT STARTS TO RISE AGAIN

As Rupert tries to get them free,
Two of the 'sweets' drop in the sea.

Salt water makes the 'sweets' bubble
As gulls ask Rupert, "What's the trouble?"

The gulls can't really understand
How Rupert's flying far from land.

And then, as Rupert starts to rise,
"What's happening in the sea?" he cries.

Over and over Rupert rolls as he tries to get the 'sweets' out of his pocket. Two of them fall into the sea before he can pop one into his mouth. At once he stops falling and when he looks down at the waves he notices something very odd. "Oh my! Those 'sweets' that fell into the sea are turning to gas already. That's only supposed to happen when they're warm. It must be something to do with the salt water. The inventor mustn't have tried them in salt water," he thinks. Now the seagulls are wondering why Rupert hasn't fallen into the sea and is still floating just above it. They fly about him squawking questions and Rupert tries to tell them about Algy and the 'sweets' and how they ate them by mistake. "My pal's up ahead of me somewhere," he says. "The breeze is stronger up there," cries one seagull. "And I do believe you are rising again." Sure enough, Rupert finds himself going up, but as he does so he looks down and sees something else rising from the sea.

RUPERT MEETS THE FLYING FISH

"I swallowed one of those small things!"
A fish cries. "Have I now got wings?"

The little bear tries to explain,
Just as the wind gets up again.

They're in a cloud, both dark and wet.
Gasps Rupert, "Ugh, how soaked I'll get!"

The sun comes out in time to show
Some tropic islands far below.

Speechless with astonishment, Rupert watches the thing pop out of the waves and float up to him. It is a large and rather frightened looking fish. "Hey, what's going on?" it gasps. "I was watching you just now and I swallowed one of those little things that dropped out of your pocket. Now look what's happened!" "Oh dear, those 'sweets' again!" cries Rupert. "And you're not even warm. Let's try to stick together and I'll explain as we're blown along. My, the wind's getting very strong?"

So Rupert explains to his strange companion all about the 'sweets' he shouldn't have swallowed as they are whisked along. But now the wind is even stronger and suddenly Rupert finds himself in the middle of a very dark, wet cloud. "Ugh, now I'm soaked!" he complains. "Nonsense, it's lovely!" exclaims the fish. "Suits me fine. Only wish it was salt water rain." But at last they reach blue skies again. "Look!" cries Rupert. "Islands. But, oh, we're too high! We'll miss them!"

RUPERT COMES DOWN TO EARTH

"I fear we'll be blown out to sea,"
Thinks Rupert. "I must grab a tree."

He holds the fish who cries, "Let go!
I much prefer the sea, you know!"

What's this? A sort of rope is thrown
Around him, tied onto a stone.

Now Rupert uses both his hands
And firmly grasps the creeper's strands.

As the islands draw nearer Rupert feels himself beginning to sink again. "Now, if the effect of the 'sweet' wears off at the right moment we can land on one of the islands," he thinks. The wind has dropped to a gentle breeze, but as Rupert and the fish drift closer and closer to the islands it looks as if they are going to be blown right over them. Then suddenly Rupert finds himself within reach of a palm tree. In an instant he has caught hold of a branch. At the same moment he grabs one of the fish's fins to save it too. "Hey, let go!" cries the fish. "I want to go down in water not on dry land!" As he lets go of the fish Rupert glances down and gasps. Strange-looking men are gathered round the base of his tree. Next minute a big stone is thrown over him and tied to it are long strands of a strong creeper. "They must be trying to get me down," thinks Rupert. "Maybe I'd better help them for I certainly can't get down by myself." He grips the strands firmly.

RUPERT IS TAKEN CAPTIVE

Now Rupert's nearly on the ground,
He thinks, "What men are these I've found?"

"They do not seem surprised that I
Should reach their island from the sky."

"I can't," cries Rupert in dismay,
"Understand one word you say!"

The leader points and, with a spear,
A fearsome-looking guard draws near.

But even as he is being pulled down Rupert is beginning to wonder about his "rescuers". They are rather fierce-looking and—yes!—some of them have swords and spears. But he can't turn back now and in a moment he finds himself seized by a big man with a dark beard. The man stares at him then says something in a strange language. All the time Rupert feels himself getting heavier as the effect of the 'sweet' disappears. Now he is beginning to feel frightened. "It's almost as if they were expecting me to come out of the sky," he thinks. "They don't seem at all surprised." He is still wondering as he is led off to a camp and made to stand on a rock while more of the fierce-looking men gather round and stare. "Oh, please," Rupert says timidly, "can't anyone speak English?" But no one says anything and they all continue to stare until the man who looks like their leader steps forward and points sternly. At once armed guards march Rupert away from the camp.

RUPERT GETS A SURPRISE

The little bear is led towards
A rock by warriors with swords.

"Oh, must I really go down there?"
Exclaims the anxious little bear.

But, guided by the light ahead,
Straight down towards the sea he's led.

Now Rupert can't believe his eyes.
"Can that be really him?" he cries.

The guards carrying swords and spears push Rupert ahead of them. They stride along so fast that the little bear has to trot to avoid being prodded by them. Nervously he keeps looking round, wondering where he is being taken and what is in store for him. After a while they reach the rocky top of a cliff. The guards make Rupert stop and then they gather round a flat stone slab. Without a word, they prise it up to reveal a hole with rough steps leading into darkness. "You can't want me to go down there, surely?" quavers Rupert. But one of the soldiers points his spear sternly and there can be no mistaking what he wants. So poor Rupert climbs into the hole and at once the slab is shut and he is left in the dark. But when his eyes are used to the dark he sees a glimmer of light ahead. Carefully he creeps down the rough steps. The light gets steadily brighter until at last he is standing at the edge of the sea among a jumble of rocks. He stops, stares and gasps.

RUPERT GREETS HIS CHUM AGAIN

"Hey, Algy!" Rupert cries. "It's me!"
His chum almost falls in the sea.

"Oh, yes, I came ahead of you.
And was brought down by creeper, too."

"We're trapped," says Algy with a sigh,
"By sea too deep and cliffs too high."

Now Algy grabs the little bear:
"I say, what's happening down there?"

Who should be sitting all alone at the end of a string of rocks and staring at the sea but Algy! Rupert gives a great whoop of delight that makes Algy jump and almost topple into the sea. "They've brought you here as well then?" he greets Rupert. "I thought they would when I saw you pulled down by those fibre ropes just as I was." The little bear gasps: "D'you mean that you were blown to this very island before me?" "Of course," Algy says. "I saw you and that fish flying over but you were so intent on catching hold of that tree that you didn't notice me." Rupert explains how the fish came to be flying and then asks, "But why have we been put down here?" "We're captives," Algy answers glumly. "This is a sort of open-air prison. The sea's behind us. The cliffs in front can't be climbed. And there's a guard at the top of that tunnel you've just come down . . . Hey, what on earth is that?" As he was speaking something caught his eye and he swings round to stare.

RUPERT HEARS SOME ADVICE

*The fish who flew cries, "Yes, it's me!
And glad to be back in the sea!"*

*"But you can go home, little bear.
Just see what's happening over there!"*

*"The wind has changed as those trees show
And it would blow you home, you know."*

*"The big fish will be told by me
To help if you come down at sea."*

At his chum's shout Rupert turns, too. "Why," he laughs, "it's my friend the fish. I say, I am so glad you're safe as well!" "Thank you," says the fish. "I drifted down just beyond the island, and was I glad to get back into the sea!" It studies the chums. "Well, how are you?" it goes on. "I thought I'd pop round and ask." Rupert sighs and says, "You're lucky you can swim. We're stuck here like prisoners." The fish looks puzzled then says, "But surely you can go home, too. Look what is

happening." And it points to the island. But though both pals stare hard they can't see what the fish means. "There's just the island," Rupert says, "and the cliffs with a guard walking up and down . . . and, oh, yes, the wind's getting stronger now." "Yes," the fish replies, "but look at the trees and the way they're being blown. The wind has turned round and would blow you back to where you came from!" And with that it flips back into the sea, leaving Rupert and Algy staring.

RUPERT IS MARCHED AWAY

"Quick, eat those things that made you fly!"
The fish exclaims. "And now, goodbye!"

The fish swims off, the two pals turn
And find a guard there, tall and stern.

Wondering what they're wanted for,
The pals are forced towards the shore.

Rupert has two 'sweets', Algy three.
They'll swallow two immediately.

The chums are still staring at where the fish disappeared when it pops up again and says, "If you have any more of those things that make you fly you'd better take them quickly. I'll warn the whales and porpoises to look out for you in case you come down too soon . . . Quick, hurry!" it finishes and dives out of sight. Rupert hears a sound behind him. He swings round and sees why the fish was urging them to hurry. One of their fierce captors has stolen up behind them. For a moment he just stares sternly then he waves his great sword towards the island. Plainly he wants the pals to go ahead of him. As the two pals pick their way up the steps Rupert says very quietly to Algy, "I've got only two of the 'sweets' left. How many have you?" "Three, I think," whispers Algy. "Let's swallow them when we have a chance." Although the fierce swordsman can't understand what they are saying, it's plain he doesn't like their talking and growls angrily.

RUPERT EATS ANOTHER "SWEET"

The guard wants one, and he's so grim
That Algy gives his last to him.

The guard, with a suspicious frown,
First tastes then gulps the last 'sweet' down.

Rupert wonders as on they trot,
"Oh, will those 'sweets' work now or not?"

The chief and his men, in dismay,
Now see the three begin to sway.

As soon as they are out in the open again, their fierce guard strides ahead to lead the pals to the camp. Behind the man's back Rupert nods to his chum and they both swallow their 'sweets'. But just as Algy is popping the second into his mouth the man swings round. He scowls and points. It's clear he wants to see a sweet. So Algy hands him his last one. Then the two pals pull out their pockets to show they have no more. The man peers at the sweet, tastes it suspiciously, then, to the chums' dismay swallows it.

Now he strides on faster than ever so that Rupert and Algy have to run to keep up. In the camp the chief and his men are waiting for the captives. But when they do come in sight something seems to be wrong. All three seem to be having difficulty in coming any nearer. The guard and the two small figures sway about and seem almost to be dancing or jumping up and down. The chief stares fiercely at the antics and shouts angrily at the three.

RUPERT AND ALGY FLY AWAY

*"Hurrah! The 'sweets' have worked once more!
We're going to fly off as before!"*

*With growing fear the guard has found
He can't keep his feet on the ground.*

*As Rupert and his chum float free,
The frightened guard clings to a tree.*

*The pals can see men gather round
To bring the guard safe to the ground.*

But, of course, Rupert, Algy and the guard can't help it. The 'sweets' they took have started to work again. "I say, that's quick!" gasps Rupert. "I know," Algy pants, "and I don't like it at all when you can't keep your feet on the ground. You can't do a thing to help yourself." "Then let's hope the wind stays in the right direction," says Rupert. By now the guard is in a panic about the mysterious thing that is happening to him. His eyes bulge and he struggles and cries out, but he only rises higher and higher. Being much lighter, Rupert and Algy rise higher and faster to where the strong wind catches them and whooshes them out over the sea. Their guard just manages to save himself by catching hold of a tree. When the chums look back they see the guard's comrades throwing up ropes to bring him down as they were fetched down. "We're lucky they weren't quick enough to try that on us again," cries Rupert. "I wonder if we shall ever find out who they are," Algy replies.

RUPERT LANDS AGAIN

The island vanishes from sight.
Now Rupert finds they're losing height.

"Look down there!" hear Rupert call.
"Dolphins and whales in case we fall!"

And now towards the land they sink.
"Can that be Sandy Bay?" they think.

Over the beach and cliffs they pass,
And Rupert grabs a tuft of grass.

By now the wind is really strong and the chums are tossed around in the air. They have a final glimpse of the islands before they find themselves among the clouds. For a long time they can't see anything, then they begin to lose height slightly. "Look down there!" calls Rupert. "All those huge fishes. Those must be the dolphins and whales our fish promised to arrange in case we fell into the sea." "What a friendly lot they must be," laughs Algy. "I must say I'm jolly glad to see them."

But the chums don't come down in the sea. Very slowly they sink towards the land that is now in sight. "I say, it's that seaside place again!" exclaims Rupert. "I really think it must be Sandy Bay." Down, down, down float the chums until just when they think they might not make it, a slightly stronger puff of wind just blows them over the top of the cliffs. Rupert is low enough now to grab a tuft of grass and stop himself from being carried any further. "Thank goodness," he sighs.

RUPERT MEETS THE WARDEN

He runs and helps his pal to land.
At first they find it hard to stand.

A man calls, "Don't move. Stay right there!
Is one of you called Rupert Bear?"

"Thank goodness you are safe and sound!
You've had us searching all around."

The puzzled man says, "Though you're small,
You seem too light—no weight at all!"

Although Rupert is down he still finds it hard to stay on the ground. But when he sees that Algy is still in the air and in danger of being blown inland, he tries to hurry after him. It is only after a breathless chase that he can grab Algy's hand and pull him down. For several minutes they cling together until they can both stand. All at once a man appears in the distance. He waves and shouts, "Hi, you youngsters. Is one of you named Rupert?" "That's me!" calls the little bear. "But how did you know? Are we near Sandy Bay? Have we been missed?" "I should say you have," comes the answer. When the man reaches them he explains that he is a Downs Warden. "I came up here to look for those odd-shaped balloons that floated over here. What luck to find you instead! Here, let me carry you back." But as he swings the chums on to his shoulders he exclaims, "How light you are. You're no weight at all!" "I know," cries Rupert, "Those weren't balloons you saw. They were us!"

RUPERT TELLS THE STORY

And now, beside the station gate,
They see their anxious parents wait.

"How did you come?" scolds Mr. Bear
"Please," Rupert says, "we came by air."

Says Mrs. Bear, "Let's have a treat.
We'll hear their story while we eat."

Their troubles haven't been in vain.
They'll never eat strange sweets again.

At the bottom of the hill the Downs Warden makes straight for Sandy Bay station. And there Rupert spies the worried figures of his Mummy and Daddy and Mrs. Pug. "Here they are!" calls the man. "A bit on the light side. I suppose they are hungry. But they seem all right, although one of them has been spinning some yarn about flying like balloons or something." "You rascals!" scolds Mr. Bear. "If you didn't come by car or train how did you get here?" "By air, truly!" says Rupert. "But please don't be angry. We didn't mean to. Somehow we got carried away." Rupert's Mummy is afraid that Mr. Bear is going to be angry so she suggests they all hear the story during a beach picnic. But when Mr. Bear has listened to the chums' adventure all he says is, "Well, I hope it's taught the pair of you a lesson." "It certainly has!" Rupert cries. "We'll never again eat sweets unless we're quite, quite sure that they're good ones." "No, never again!" promises his chum.

RUPERT and the SILENT DOG

"Look at that dog!" cries Rupert Bear,
"He's shopping in the store, just there."

The clever dog runs up a hill,
"Let's follow him awhile," says Bill.

Rupert and Bill have had a long walk to a neighbouring village. Having been there only a few times before, they do not know the place very well, so they are having a good look round. They find the village store almost empty, but to their surprise see a large dog with a sort of belt to which are attached two leather bags. "Look at that dog, Bill," whispers Rupert, "have you seen anything like it?" Bill doesn't answer immediately, for at that moment the dog has placed a basket in front of the shopkeeper.

The man bends down and picks up a written list and, after studying it, he loads up the leather bags and the basket with groceries. At last, satisfied that he has missed nothing, he takes the money and places the change in the basket. As soon as he has heard the coins slide into the accustomed place, the dog solemnly lifts the basket and walks straight past the pals and rapidly sets off up a slope. "What a wonderful creature he is," says Bill. "Come on, Rupert, let's follow and see where he goes to."

RUPERT AND BILL ON THE TRAIL

A heavy shower begins to fall.
They cannot see the dog at all.

The chums seek shelter from the rain,
And there they meet the dog again.

They speak to him—he pays no heed;
But just looks very fierce indeed.

The rain stops suddenly once more,
And off the dog goes, as before.

Rupert is as inquisitive as Bill. "I certainly would like to know where he is going and who he belongs to," he says. They hurry up the slope, but as soon as they reach the high ground a sharp shower of rain begins. "We've missed him," says Bill. "He has disappeared. Let's take shelter for a minute." As they push into a thick bush they realize that a pair of serious eyes are fixed on them. "It's the dog! He's sheltering with us," cries Rupert. "Good doggie! Where are you going? Whose are you?"

The dog keeps quite silent and does not move. "Let's see if he has a name on his collar," says Rupert, edging forward, but at that the strange animal turns his head ever so slightly, his eyes narrow and his top lip curls up menacingly, though he still does not make a sound. The two pals draw back hurriedly. "He looks as if he'll bite," says Bill shakily. However, nothing happens. The shower soon stops and the dog, picking up his basket, leaves the bushes and walks sedately away.

RUPERT SHELTERS HIS PAL

"I think we'd better go," says Bill,
But Rupert wants to follow still.

So on they go, until they find,
The dog has stopped, with rocks behind.

But now they have a nasty shock,
The dog dives at them from a rock.

Bill tumbles over in his fright,
But Rupert stops the dog's mad flight.

When the dog has gone Bill thinks it's time to go home. "He doesn't seem to like us," he says. "He didn't wag his tail." "No, but he didn't growl, either," answers Rupert. "I'm still too inquisitive about him. He's such a clever creature." So they push on up the hill to where the surface becomes very rough. "Look!" cries the little bear, "the dog can't get any farther. There are only tall rocks beyond him." As he speaks the dog turns his head and gazes at them from behind a boulder.

Next moment the dog lowers his basket and without the slightest warning doubles round the boulder and bears down on them at a great rate. "Look out, he's coming for us!" gasps Bill. Turning to run he trips over a stone and falls headlong. Rupert sees that his pal is down and, with no time to think, steps across to shield him. The dog, taken by surprise, skids violently to a halt and for an instant they face each other. Meanwhile Bill is able to scramble to his feet.

RUPERT DECIDES TO EXPLORE

The strange dog leans towards the bear,
Then waves his front paw in the air.

"Well!" Rupert gasps, "I'm going on.
I really must know where he's gone."

The dog has disappeared again,
But there's one path that is quite plain.

A dark cave opens on the right,
But still the dog is not in sight.

After a short pause the strange dog leans his head towards the little bear and again his top lip curls up hardly showing his teeth. Then with a wave of his paw he returns to pick up his basket. "Whew, what an escape!" cries Bill. "Come, let's run." But Rupert stares in perplexity. "He really is the oddest creature," he says. "I declare he was grinning at me that time! I simply must find out where he's going." He climbs cautiously to the boulder while Bill follows very gingerly.

Beyond the boulder Rupert finds himself in a rough passage with more boulders on one side and higher rocks on the other. Just before the passage comes to a dead end he spies a dark tunnel on the right. "The dog must have gone in there," he murmurs; "there's nowhere else for him to go." He peers in but can only see as far as the first bend. "I wish it were not all so silent," he says. "I'm going to explore a little way. Wait for me, Bill." And in he goes on all fours.

RUPERT SENDS BILL FOR HELP

An iron door shuts behind the bear,
And he is really trapped in there.

He crawls into the larger place,
And, with the dog, comes face to face.

Now Rupert sees a man there too,
And thinks, "He'll tell me what to do."

The man looks cross and fiercely scowls,
"Why did you come in here?" he growls.

Rupert has barely reached the first bend when there is a loud clang behind him. An iron door has dropped through a slot in the rock and has shut him in. He beats on it and can faintly hear the voice of Bill beyond. "Go for help, I'm caught in here!" calls Rupert. And crawling slowly round the bend he finds he is at the entrance of a large cave while, sitting facing him, is the dog. For three minutes the dog gazes at him, silent as ever, then it turns and Rupert can only follow.

The dog walks up to a rather untidy old gentleman who is sitting on a stool. "Oh, please, will you show me how to get out?" says Rupert nervously. "I've got shut in. I didn't mean to break into your home, if this is your home." The man gazes at him in a curious way. "Then what did you mean?" he growls. "I knew you were coming. My dog showed you as plainly as he could that he didn't want you, and still you come. Inquisitive, that's what you are, and now you must pay for it!"

RUPERT WANTS SIX LETTERS

And then he says, "I've peep-holes here,
So I can see who's coming near."

Then Rupert's asked to help the man
Complete his crossword, if he can.

He needs a word with "H" begun,
But Rupert cannot think of one.

So while the man stares at the floor,
The little bear creeps to a door.

Rupert is taken by surprise. "But please tell me," he says, "how could you know I was coming when you were sitting here?" "I have peep-holes through the rock on all sides like that one," answers the man gruffly. "I know everything that goes on. And now, no more questions. Come and help me. I'm making up a crossword and I want a word of six letters beginning with H." Feeling still more surprised Rupert kneels and sees that there are markings on a sandy part of the floor of the cave.

Getting to his feet Rupert looks round in a bewildered way. "Come on, come on," says the man harshly. "Six letters beginning with H." Rupert scratches his head and tries to think. "Oh dear, I'm not much good at spelling," he mutters, walking slowly round the cave. All at once he spies a doorway beyond an angle of rock and his hopes revive. He glances back. The man and the silent dog are intent on the crossword and do not seem to be noticing him. Gently he tries the handle.

RUPERT HEARS OF THE HERMIT

To his delight it opens wide,
And Rupert quickly slips outside.

The path ends suddenly, and so
There's no way to the rocks below.

Some birds fly round the little bear,
And ask him what he's doing there.

They say, "That man is very kind,
His little joke you must not mind."

To Rupert's great joy the door opens without a sound and ahead of him he sees another tunnel with daylight at the end of it. "This is wonderful," he breathes. "I can escape from, this mad place after all!" He tiptoes forward and then stops abruptly, for below him is a steep drop. He gazes around and realizes that the tunnel is just a hole in a great cliff. There is no way of climbing either up or down. As he pauses lots of birds swoop in to look at him.

Some large birds fly round him screeching hungrily and are followed by a flock of smaller ones. "Hello," chirps a sparrow. "Who are you? You're looking pretty glum." "I'm trying to get away from that awful old man," says Rupert miserably. "Hey, don't you go calling· him names!" cheeps another sparrow. "He's a lovely old man. He's a hermit and he has a dog who does all his shopping for him, and he loves birds and he feeds us every day but he does like to be left alone."

RUPERT GIVES SIX LETTERS

"The man's a hermit," says a bird,
And Rupert thinks, "is that the word?"

It starts with "H", so that will do,
And there are five more letters, too.

So Rupert goes back to the man,
And speaks as bravely as he can.

The hermit looks at him awhile,
Then slowly, he begins to smile.

Rupert is astonished. "Are you sure that's all true?" he asks. "Of course it is," says the sparrow. "He's even trained his dog not to bark for fear of frightening us. And he's a hermit because he wants quiet for making his crosswords. But he does love to tease people who are inquisitive. Perhaps that is why you are feeling so glum!" Rupert stares in relief. "So that explains everything!" he breathes. Then an idea strikes him. "Hermit! Surely that has six letters and it starts with H!"

The sparrows are so sure of what they are saying that Rupert decides to go back. Re-entering the cave he faces the old gentleman as bravely as he can. "Please, I believe you've been teasing me all the time," he says. "I'm sorry if I was inquisitive. I didn't mean any harm. And, please, is 'hermit' the word you want for your crossword?" The man and the silent dog look at him solemnly for a moment. Then they both break into a smile and the man begins to chuckle.

RUPERT HAS AFTERNOON TEA

He says, "I like you, little bear,
You are most difficult to scare."

And now this rather curious three,
Sit down together and have tea.

The hermit says, "You must not stay;
My dog will take you on your way."

They leave by yet another door,
That Rupert has not seen before.

"Oho, so a little bird has been telling you my secrets, has he?" laughs the old man. "Well, well it's quite true. I don't want visitors and I could have pulled a lever and shut that iron door before you got in, but I had watched you on the hillside and I liked the way you stood up to my dog when he rushed at you and pretended to be fierce, so I allowed you to come in in spite of your inquisitiveness. Now let's have tea and you shall tell me your name."

Rupert is delighted at the way things have turned out and he tells the old gentleman his name and all about himself. "It's a topping cave you have here," he says. "And I wish I knew how you trained this wonderful dog. May I bring my pal to see you?" "No, you certainly may not," smiles the old man. "You've disturbed me enough already. So now good-bye." The dog rises at once to lead Rupert away through yet another rocky tunnel.

RUPERT TELLS HIS STORY

"Where am I now?" asks Rupert—but
At once the heavy door is shut.

Just then Bill Badger comes in sight,
Relieved to find his chum all right.

A farm-hand kindly came along,
To help in case things had gone wrong.

But all has ended happily,
As Bill and Rupert both agree.

When he reaches the open air Rupert gazes around. "Please how do I get back to where I entered?" he asks. But the only answer is a loud clang. Another iron door has dropped suddenly and the dog has disappeared. Rather anxiously he climbs to a higher point and down below him he spies his pal Bill Badger. "Oh, Rupert, are you safe?" cries Bill breathlessly. "I couldn't find a policeman, but this farm worker heard what happened and has come to help you. Do tell how you got out."

The farm-hand doesn't wait to be told. "You've bin meetin' our silent dawg, I'll be bound," he laughs. "And I'll lay he's led you a pretty dance. But I see he's done you no harm. He never does. So I'll leave you and get back to my work." He says good-bye and Rupert takes the arm of his pal. "It's high time we went home," he smiles. "We do meet some odd people on our walks and the old hermit certainly was funny. Come on and I'll tell you all about it."

RUPERT and the Baby Cloud

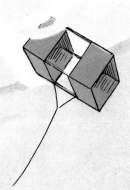

The strong wind tugs at Rupert's kite,
"Look out!" calls Algy. "Hold on tight!"

IT is a windy day with grey clouds scudding across the sky, and Rupert sets off to sail his kite. "I'll look for a spot where there aren't any large trees," he thinks. Soon he finds just the right place on top of a hill.

He unwinds the string and as he launches his kite the wind lifts it into the air. The little bear is so busy that he does not notice Algy running towards him.

At that moment a strong gust of wind lifts the kite still higher, carrying Rupert off the ground! "Hang on, I'm coming," yells Algy. Racing up, he grabs Rupert and pulls with all his might.

When Rupert Bear is carried up,
He's quickly rescued by the pup.

RUPERT LOOKS INSIDE HIS KITE

With Algy's help it's not so hard,
They haul the kite in yard by yard.

Then Rupert stares and gives a cry—
"A cloud has come down from the sky!"

The little cloud holds so much rain,
It cannot float back home again.

From high above a cloud looks down,
And Algy's sure he sees it frown!

The little pup manages to get Rupert back to the ground. "Whew! Thanks, Algy," gasps Rupert. "You were just in time." They haul in the string and soon the kite is lying beside them. "Look, Algy, there's something inside it," cries Rupert. The two chums peer closely and there, trapped inside the kite, is a tiny grey cloud. "Goodness, how did it get in there?" gasps Algy. "The wind must have blown it inside," says Rupert, and he shakes the kite to free the little cloud.

Rupert lifts the cloud expecting it to float away, but it sinks to the ground. "I think I know the reason," he sighs. "It is heavy with rain. You can tell by the colour, it's such a dark grey. I'd better take it home with me. We can't leave it here." Algy carries the kite while his chum carefully holds the cloud. "Poor thing," says Rupert, "it's just a baby." Then Algy calls out: "Rupert, I believe one of the big clouds is frowning at us for taking the little cloud away. We'd better hurry."

RUPERT SETS THE CLOUD FREE

His story of the baby cloud,
Makes Edward blink and gasp aloud.

"That's right," says Mummy with a smile,
"Just leave the cloud to soak awhile."

"It's white as snow," says Rupert Bear,
"And see—it's floating in the air!"

They go outside. "I'll set it free,
Now watch," laughs Rupert gleefully.

"I don't think you should have run off with it like that," grumbles Edward, "just when I was blowing my biggest bubbles." But Rupert soon puts matters right by explaining about the Cloud-scrubber and the baby cloud. When they arrive at the cottage they go into the kitchen. "Will you do some washing for me, Mummy?" asks Rupert. "Of course, dear," answers Mrs. Bear. "There is plenty of hot water." Rupert fetches the baby cloud from his bedroom, and Edward watches him dip it in the sink.

"The Cloud-scrubber said that he used this special soap to clean the clouds, so it should be all right for this baby cloud," murmurs Rupert. When Mrs. Bear returns she begins to wash the cloud. Before long its greyness disappears and it becomes white and fluffy. "My! How light it is," says Mrs. Bear. "Now we can take it into the garden and let it float away," says Rupert happily. He carries the little cloud outside and throws it into the air. It rises slowly, tinged pink by the rays of the sun.

RUPERT RECEIVES A MESSAGE

Up goes the cloud, yet higher still,
The sight gives both the chums a thrill.

Then to the kite the soap is tied.
Says Rupert, "It's quite safe inside."

They hope the idea hasn't failed,
When high aloft the kite has sailed.

The words of thanks are all they need,
To make them pleased with their good deed!

The chums watch for a long time as the cloud floats higher and higher until it joins company with a passing cloud. "Now what's Rupert up to?" thinks Edward as his chum suddenly hurries indoors. In a few moments Rupert is back with his kite and a small parcel. "I've wrapped the soap in this parcel and if we tie it inside the kite we can send it back to my friend the Cloud-scrubber," he explains to Edward. "That big cloud overhead is where he is likely to be."

Presently the kite is hidden in the cloud above them. "I hope he is there," murmurs Rupert. After a while they pull the kite down and the parcel is no longer in it. "So the Cloud-scrubber must have taken the soap," says Edward. "And just look, he has written a message." On the side of the kite in big letters are the words THANK YOU. At that moment Algy comes running up the garden path. "We've got lots to talk about. Come inside and we'll tell you everything," laughs Rupert.